# Things That Go

Illustrated by **Ethel Gold**

Ladybird Books

**red**

bicycle

car

fire engine

orange

cement mixer

bulldozer

sailboat

yellow

school bus

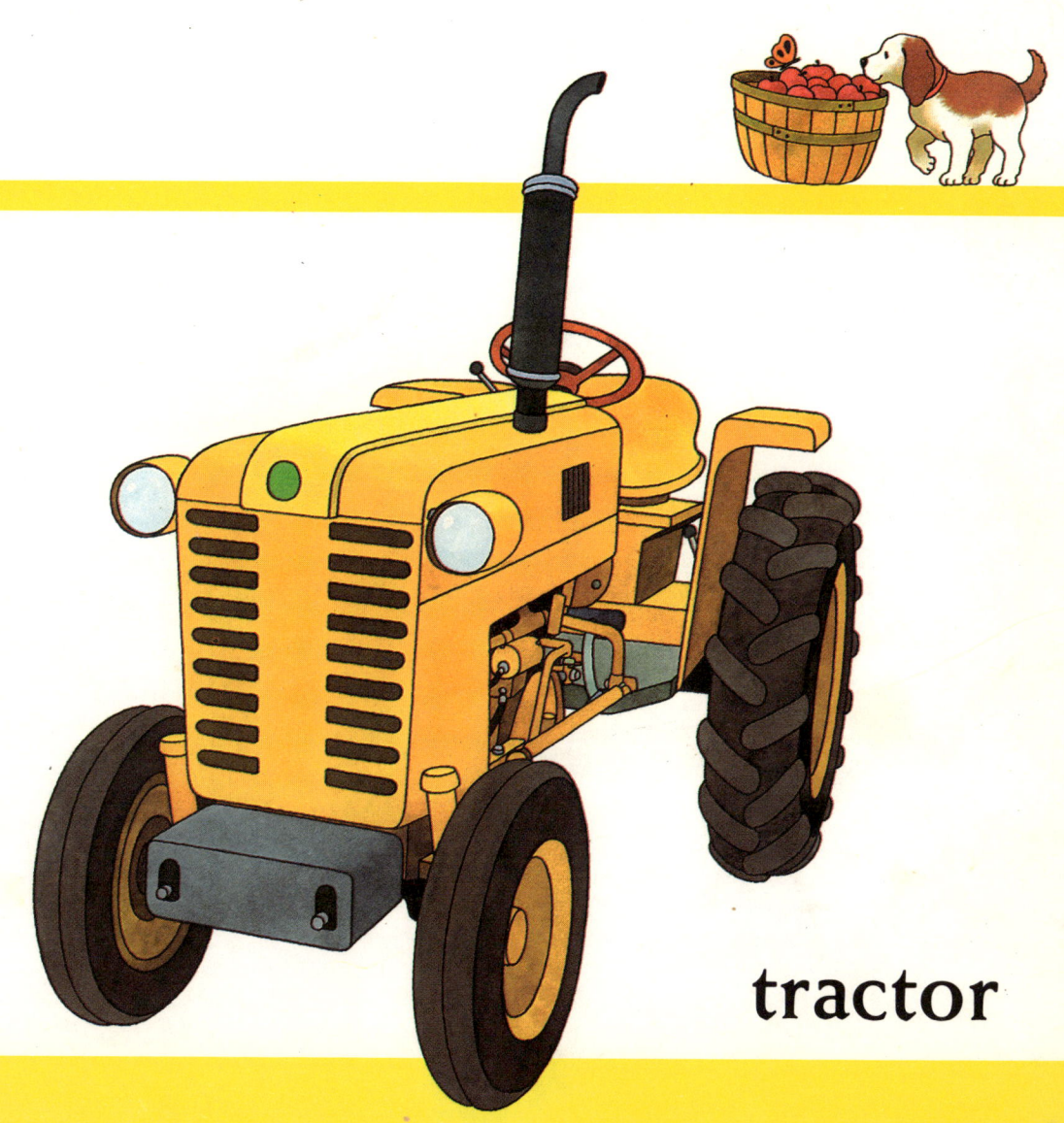

tractor

trolley

taxi

## green

submarine

**train**

jeep

**garbage truck**

**airplane**

motorcycle

**van**

tricycle

ferry

**speedboat**